MW01102689

CLAIRE AINSLIE

MINNEAPOLIS

Darby Creek
A division of Lerner Publishing Group, Inc.
241 First Avenue North
Minneapolis, MN 55401 USA

For reading levels and more information, look up this title at www.lernerbooks.com.

Image credits: Ostill/Shutterstock.com; vlastas/Shutterstock.com; Banan/Shutterstock.com.

Main body text set in Janson Text LT Std 12/17.5.
Typeface provided by Adobe Systems.

Library of Congress Cataloging-in-Publication Data

Names: Ainslie, Claire, 1992– author.
Title: The One / Claire Ainslie.
Description: Minneapolis : Darby Creek, 2019. | Series: Reality show | Summary: As a cast member of the reality dating show, The One, sixteen-year-old Charlotte is determined to prove that the program is fake, but her plan goes awry when she falls for Dominic, the show's main love interest.
Identifiers: LCCN 2018014396 (print) | LCCN 2018020308 (ebook) | ISBN 9781541541894 (eb pdf) | ISBN 9781541540262 (lb : alk. paper) | ISBN 9781541545434 (pb : alk. paper)
Subjects: | CYAC: Dating (Social customs)—Fiction. | Reality television programs—Fiction.
Classification: LCC PZ7.1.A365 (ebook) | LCC PZ7.1.A365 On 2019 (print) | DDC [Fic]—dc23

LC record available at https://lccn.loc.gov/2018014396

Manufactured in the United States of America
1-45231-36613-8/9/2018

For my parents, who gave me the
joy of books and believe in me more
than I believe in myself

CHAPTER 1

"I don't know why you like this show so much," said Charlotte. For the third time that afternoon, the theme music for *The One* played from the TV.

Madeline, her best friend, rolled her eyes. "Because it's romantic!" she said, sighing a little. "Plus, the guys are always so gorgeous! I mean, haven't you been paying any attention? Andy's eyes are so nice. And his hair. Don't even get me started on his hair."

Charlotte laughed. "I'll give you that—he has good hair. But it's all so fake! How can anyone fall in love while you're being filmed?

Especially when the guy is dating three other girls at the same time!" She shook her head. "They're only in it for the attention. Not to mention the promise ring and the scholarship."

The winner of the show got a promise ring and a $50,000 scholarship to put toward college. But Charlotte thought most of the contestants seemed more interested in the promise ring.

"Don't you want to go live in a beautiful house on Cliff Lake for the summer?" Madeline continued. "And they always get to go on awesome dates. Who gets to go up in a hot air balloon for a date at sixteen?"

"No one," said Charlotte, flipping her long, dark hair over her shoulder. "But that's exactly my point—the show isn't based in reality. How are you going to know if you get along with him in real life? I just don't see how it can work."

"Well, even if it didn't work, it would be so much fun while it lasted!" said Madeline.

"You're such a romantic," said Charlotte, smiling.

"I know," Madeline giggled. "Now shut up—we're going to miss it!" They turned back to the TV.

At the next commercial break, an ad for the show came on. "Do you want the chance to meet the love of your life?" asked a deep voice. "Send in your application for *The One* today for a chance to date Dominic!" A dark-haired guy with a wide smile appeared on the screen. Charlotte had to admit that he was cute, but he looked like he knew it. They showed footage of him playing with a golden retriever and playing soccer. He was wearing a cutoff T-shirt, with his arm muscles on full display.

"Come on," said Charlotte, rolling her eyes. "Who even signs up for this stuff?"

"Uh . . ." said Madeline, a guilty smile on her face.

"No!" said Charlotte, sitting straight up. "You didn't! What about Ben?" Madeline had been dating Ben for six months. Before that it was John, and before that, Max. Charlotte couldn't remember the last time her best friend had been single for more than a couple weeks.

"Of course I didn't! I've got a guy!" Madeline said. Charlotte suddenly felt her stomach drop. She thought she knew where this was going. "You, on the other hand . . ." Madeline stared innocently at the ceiling.

"You did not!" shrieked Charlotte, suddenly panicking. "Why would you do that?"

"You need to get out more! Have some fun!" said Madeline. "All you ever do is study or train for soccer. You're missing out. Going on the show would be good for you." Madeline paused. "Plus he likes soccer, and you like soccer! He could be your perfect match!"

Ignoring the last part, Charlotte said, "Missing out on what? Sweaty hand-holding at a crappy movie? Crying in the bathroom during lunch because some guy dumped me at school?" She narrowed her eyes and glared at Madeline. "No thanks."

"I only cried through lunch that one time!" protested Madeline. "And you're missing out on having someone to talk to and hang out with."

"I don't see why I need a guy for any of that. Besides, I'll have plenty of time for guys after I've gotten into college."

"Fine, but I hope they pick you," said Madeline. "You could meet the guy of your dreams, go on some awesome dates, and pay for college!"

"I'll take out loans," said Charlotte stubbornly, but she smiled. "They aren't going to pick me anyway. I bet hundreds of people apply."

"You never know," replied Madeline with a shrug.

The show was back on, and one of the girls was crying in her confessional. Charlotte wasn't paying attention anymore, though. She couldn't believe Madeline had applied for her without even asking. She was a little annoyed, but she didn't think they'd pick her anyway. There were only four contestants, after all. The chance of her being one of them was tiny. And she could always say no.

Could I really say no, though? she wondered suddenly. *That scholarship is too big to pass up.* She turned her attention back to *The One*. Even if it wasn't real, it was entertaining—and it was nice to think about something other than school for once. Soccer practice started on Monday, and she wouldn't have any free time again until June.

Charlotte and Madeline watched the entire season, giggling at the way a girl hung on Andy's arm as he tried to show her how to play the guitar. "If they pick you," said Madeline, "please don't act like that!"

Charlotte looked offended. "Of course not! It's pathetic! You'd think he was the only guy left on Earth."

"And he looks annoyed," said Madeline. "I'll bet it gets old after a while, even if he likes the attention at the beginning."

"I bet the producers tell the girls to act like that," said Charlotte.

"Well, if you're picked, you can tell me," replied Madeline.

Charlotte just rolled her eyes.

***

Charlotte stepped out of the steamy shower and sighed. The water had felt good on her sore muscles. The first week of practice was always tough, but she loved the feeling of pushing her body to the limit. She wrapped herself in a towel and padded quietly to her room.

She dressed in a pair of comfortable sweatpants and an old T-shirt and flopped down on the bed, checking her phone. To Charlotte's surprise, she had a missed call and voicemail from an unfamiliar number. She had to listen to it three times before she was sure it wasn't Madeline playing a trick on her.

"Charlotte," said a woman's brisk voice, "I'm calling to inform you that you've been selected to appear on the next season of *The One*. Please return this call to confirm you are still interested. Filming begins the third week of June and will finish at the end of July. We will only hold your spot for forty-eight hours. If we don't hear from you, it will be given to the next alternate on the list."

Charlotte stared at her phone, her mouth hanging open. *This can't be happening*, she thought. No matter how much she and Madeline joked about it, she never imagined there was any chance they'd actually choose her. To go on television. On a *dating show*, of all things.

She groaned and flipped onto her stomach, burying her face in the pillows. That was the part that scared her—the dating part. She didn't really have any experience with guys, which didn't usually bother her. She figured she would have plenty of time to date later. But having her first dating experiences on national television was not how she expected things to happen.

Still, going on *The One* would give her the opportunity to try things she wouldn't get a chance to do otherwise. She doubted she'd fall in love in six weeks, but maybe Madeline had a point about putting herself out there and having some fun. Plus, she really couldn't turn down the chance for a $50,000 scholarship.

She took a deep breath and called the producer back. The line only rang once before a businesslike voice answered, "Yes?"

"Hi, I just got a call about appearing on *The One*," said Charlotte. "My name is Charlotte James."

"Ah yes, Ms. James. My name is Catherine. I'm the head producer on the show. We want to offer you a position in the cast for this summer if you're still interested."

"I am, thank you for the offer."

The woman on the other end paused, as if waiting for more of a response. Charlotte cleared her throat and then said, "I'm so excited!" She cringed at the fake enthusiasm.

"Excellent. We'll send a contract and information packet to the address provided on your application. We look forward to having you with us this summer." Catherine sounded like she was reciting a speech she'd given many times. She hung up the phone before Charlotte could say anything else.

CHAPTER

2

As she stepped off the plane a few weeks later,
Charlotte still couldn't believe her mom had
said yes to this. It had taken some convincing,
but ultimately the possibility of winning the
scholarship had won her over.

A driver took Charlotte to the network's
headquarters, where she would meet the
producer and other contestants before traveling
to the set. There, a receptionist guided her into
a conference room with beautiful views over
the city. After about five minutes she heard
the door open, and the receptionist was back,
followed by a girl with straight black hair. She

had blunt bangs across her forehead and the biggest smile Charlotte had ever seen.

"This is Charlotte," said the receptionist, gesturing to her. "Charlotte, this is—"

"I'm Olivia," she said enthusiastically. She bounced across the room and hugged Charlotte, who froze—she wasn't really a hugger. "I can't wait to get started!" gushed Olivia. "Isn't this amazing? This is going to be the best summer!"

"I'll leave you two to chat," said the receptionist, backing out of the room.

Olivia didn't seem to notice that Charlotte hadn't spoken yet. "Isn't Dominic gorgeous? I can't wait to meet him! He looks just like his dad, all that dark hair, and those intense eyes . . ." she sighed dramatically.

"How do you know he looks like his dad?" asked Charlotte, confused. She'd seen a picture of Dominic—who was definitely good-looking—and had thought he'd looked familiar. She couldn't figure out why, though.

"Seriously?" said Olivia, raising an eyebrow. "You don't know who he is?"

Charlotte just shook her head.

"His dad is Darren Mackenzie. He's won three Oscars! You know, big action star?"

"Really? I had no idea," said Charlotte. *I guess that explains it.*

Before Olivia could respond, the receptionist was back with two new girls.

"Teagan and Delaney," said the receptionist, gesturing to each of them.

Olivia immediately introduced herself while Charlotte watched from her spot near the windows. Teagan walked in like she owned the building. She was tall and curvy, with perfectly curled hair and a very trendy outfit. Delaney had unruly curly hair that partially covered her eyes, and she watched Teagan like she was trying to learn how to be just like her.

They'd all said hello and were looking curiously at each other when the door opened again. The woman who walked through it was more glamorous than anyone Charlotte had ever seen in real life.

"You've all met? Good," she said without waiting for any of them to answer. "I'm

Catherine, the head producer for *The One*. You four were chosen out of thousands of girls because we think you could all be good fits for this season's young man, Dominic. Remember this is TV, and we expect you all to be your best, most interesting selves during filming.

"Now, for the rules. You'll be housed near the lodge on Cliff Lake. You'll all be sharing a cabin, so you'd better get used to each other. You are not to see Dominic unless you are on camera. Anyone who breaks this rule will be in serious trouble and could be sent home. It's important for the integrity of the show that the audience gets to see all of your interactions with him, so viewers at home can see this is the real deal. You'll also need to give us your phones. We can't have you spoiling the show for the audience if you talk to your friends at home.

"You'll all have a group date and a one-on-one date with Dominic each week, and you'll film confessionals every week. These will be your chance to express your feelings about Dominic and your fellow contestants. We will head out to the lake right away. Filming begins tomorrow."

Catherine swept out of the room without another word. The receptionist poked her head through the door and beckoned them all. "Let's go, ladies," she said. "There's a van waiting downstairs."

***

The drive to Cliff Lake took three hours. Olivia didn't shut up until Teagan finally snapped that she was getting a headache. Delaney slept the whole way. Charlotte spent the drive looking out the window, watching the hills get bigger as they drove into the mountains. She was too nervous to sleep.

Finally the van stopped at a wooded campground. Several small cabins stood off to the side, and there was a larger building on the other side of a small clearing. It didn't look anything like Charlotte had seen on TV—she didn't see the lodge anywhere.

"Are we staying *here*?" Teagan whispered to Delaney before they stepped out of the van.

Teagan sounded offended, but Charlotte didn't think it looked that bad. It just wasn't fancy.

Catherine was there to meet them. She led them into the large building, which turned out to be a common area.

"This is where you'll eat any meals that aren't part of filming," said Catherine, pointing through a set of double doors to a small dining hall.

"Excuse me," said Teagan, "but where is the lodge? I didn't sign up to go to summer camp like a ten-year-old."

Charlotte thought this would annoy Catherine, but she just smiled. "You'll see the lodge when filming begins. Unfortunately, you won't be living there. The owner allows us to film inside, but he won't let a bunch of teenagers live in his house without supervision. I think you'll find your housing to be just fine."

"We'd better not have to use an outhouse," said Teagan, sulking.

"No, there's a bathroom in your cabin," said Catherine.

Teagan still looked upset, but Catherine

plowed on, "Go get settled in." She pointed out
the window to where a driver was unloading
their luggage. "Decide what you want to wear
tomorrow to meet Dominic. And figure out
how you're going to make yourselves stand out.
Charlotte, could I speak to you?"

Charlotte walked across the room, curious.

"I'd like to know if we can call you Charlie
during filming," said Catherine. "Charlotte is
just such a *stuffy* name." She wrinkled her nose.

Charlotte was shocked. She'd never had
a nickname, and she'd never wanted one.
Charlotte suited her. *Charlie* was a bubbly,
outgoing girl she didn't know. Charlie wasn't
an ambitious student and soccer player. "I don't
think—"

"Excellent!" said Catherine, patting her
shoulder and smiling like Charlotte had
agreed. "Charlie it is!" Catherine walked away
before she had a chance to argue.

Grumbling to herself, Charlotte followed
the other girls toward their cabin. As she passed
Catherine and the group of production staff,
Charlotte heard Catherine say, "Make sure

you get a lot of good footage of Teagan. She's obviously the strong contender here. I can't imagine Dominic going for the mouse, the nerd, or the girl who thinks she farts rainbows."

I knew it, thought Charlotte. *No one thinks I can win. I guess I'll just have to prove them wrong.*

CHAPTER

3

The next morning, Charlotte was woken
by someone knocking loudly on the door.
Catherine's voice was muffled as she yelled,
"Time to get up, girls! You have two hours to
get ready!"

Charlotte groaned and sat up. Her nerves
were already twisting her stomach into knots,
but she tried to ignore it. It wouldn't do any
good to freak out now. Teagan climbed down
from the upper bunk above Delaney and rushed
to the bathroom, slamming the door behind her.

"Hurry, I've got to go," called Olivia, though
she was smiling, as usual. Teagan didn't answer.

Charlotte climbed out of bed and opened her suitcase. She pulled out jeans and a plain T-shirt. Catherine never said they were supposed to dress up, and Charlotte hadn't brought that many fancy clothes anyway.

After she got dressed, she pulled out the small makeup bag Madeline had filled for her and sighed. Charlotte didn't really like wearing makeup, but since she was being filmed, she figured she'd need to wear at least a little. Holding the makeup bag and her toothbrush, she knocked on the bathroom door.

"Teagan, are you almost done? The rest of us need to use the bathroom too."

"Well, you'll just have to wait," Teagan snapped.

"Someone's not a morning person!" sang Olivia.

Even though she was annoyed with Teagan, Charlotte winced. She wasn't a morning person either, and Olivia's cheeriness grated.

"I'm enough of a morning person to get the bathroom first," said Teagan. The door opened just a bit. "Delaney, get in here!" called Teagan.

"You can help with my hair."

Delaney slid into the bathroom without looking at anyone.

Charlotte just sighed. It wasn't worth fighting about. "Come on," she said to Olivia. "We'll go get breakfast first. Maybe they'll be done when we get back."

***

When they returned, the bathroom was finally free. Teagan had on an outfit that Charlotte thought was completely impractical for the woods—a bright red crop top and a short black skirt. She had, at least, put on sneakers instead of one of the many pairs of heels she'd brought with her. Delaney was wearing denim shorts and a tank top. They had both gone all out on their hair and makeup.

"You're wearing *that*?" asked Teagan, pointing at Charlotte's simple outfit.

Charlotte shrugged and raised an eyebrow. "This is how I dress," she said.

"To do what, mow your lawn?" said Delaney, snickering.

Delaney had said so little that Charlotte was surprised to hear her say something at all, let alone something nasty. "Sometimes," was all she said back.

"I think she looks fine," said Olivia. "The point of this show is for us to be ourselves and see who has the best connection with Dominic. If she wants him to actually like her, she should dress like she would at home."

"I'm not so sure Catherine cares if we're ourselves," said Charlotte, frowning. "Or she wouldn't insist on calling me Charlie."

"It's cute!" said Olivia.

"But it's not my name! It doesn't fit me."

"Yeah, I wouldn't say you're cute," said Teagan nastily. Delaney laughed behind her hand.

"I don't need to be cute," said Charlotte. She walked into the bathroom, looked into the mirror, and took a deep breath. Though she wouldn't let Teagan and Delaney see it, they had hurt her feelings a little. She was already anxious enough about meeting Dominic for the first time, but she did her best to ignore the girls' snide remarks. Letting them get under her skin would only make things worse.

As annoying as Charlotte found Olivia, at least Olivia wouldn't try to convince her to act like someone else. She couldn't do that, even to try to win the scholarship. Either Dominic would like her or he wouldn't.

CHAPTER
4

Twenty minutes later, a production assistant collected them. The van only drove for five minutes. When it stopped, Teagan leaned forward and poked the driver. "Is this it? I don't see anything."

"Right through there," he said, pointing through a small gap in the trees. "You'll all be going in separately, so we'll stop here for now."

The van door opened and Catherine waved them all out. "Let's go, girls! Teagan, you're first, then Delaney. Charlie third, Olivia last. You've only got one take to make a true first impression! Make it count."

Charlotte and the others stood by the car to wait as Teagan walked through the trees and out of sight. She was glad she couldn't see anything. It would just make her more nervous.

Fifteen minutes later, the cameras reappeared, and then Delaney took her turn. When the scene was reset for Charlotte, she took a deep breath. *Just going to say hi to a normal guy*, she thought, slowly walking through the trees.

The lodge was huge. A curved staircase surrounded by flowers led up to the giant front door. Windows filled the three-story wall, and Charlotte could see all the way through the great room and out the windows on the back wall to the sparkling lake.

Behind her Catherine hissed, "Don't forget to smile, Charlie!"

Wiping her sweaty hands on her jeans, Charlotte walked up the stairs. She tried to smile, but she was sure she looked nervous. There was a camera in her face as soon as she reached the landing. Another camera followed her movements from behind.

The door to the lodge was heavy, but it swung open easily. Dominic stood in the entryway, dressed in jeans and a T-shirt with a blazer over the top. He looked relaxed, even with the cameras and producers everywhere. His dark hair was wavy and gelled back. His eyes twinkled as he grinned at her.

Charlotte's heart started to race. *He's even cuter in person*, she thought in spite of herself.

"Hi," he said, smiling confidently at her. "I'm Dominic. Welcome to the lodge." He pulled her in for a quick hug, and she had to fight not to flinch. Surprisingly, it didn't bother her as much this time. The butterflies in her stomach fluttered and she let go quickly, flustered.

"I'm, um, Charlie," she said, only hesitating a second before using the nickname. "Nice to meet you." She plastered a smile on her face, hoping she looked more relaxed than she felt.

"What, no singing? No joke? No cartwheel?" he said, laughing a little. "Not even a one-liner? I thought Teagan was going to blow out her mic with the song she sang."

"Not really my thing," she said, shrugging. Even the thought of pulling a stunt like Teagan's was mortifying to her.

"What is your thing?" he asked, tilting his head to the side.

"I guess you'll have to wait and see," she said. Her smile was real this time, though her tone was still frosty. She winced internally. She didn't mean to sound rude, she was just uncomfortable. Dominic looked so at ease and all she wanted to do was run.

"A mystery," he said, winking at her. "I like that."

Charlotte avoided his eyes. She could feel herself blushing and she twisted her fingers together nervously. *Get a grip*, she thought. *He's probably full of himself. Who else would come on a show like this?* She glanced up from under her lashes to find him still looking at her. For a second he looked curious, but then the confident smirk was back.

Feeling more and more uncomfortable, Charlotte reminded herself of the scholarship. She'd already decided not to pretend to be someone she wasn't to win it, but it was the only thing keeping her there with the cameras focused on her every move. She could only hope Dominic would turn out to be nicer than she expected.

The silence seemed to go on and on, with neither Charlotte nor Dominic sure what to do next. Finally Catherine put them out of their misery.

"Cut!" yelled Catherine. "Charlie, head through to the great room and wait quietly with the others."

Half an hour later, all four girls were gathered in the great room. Olivia's giggling over Dominic stopped when he, Catherine, and the camera crew walked in. "You have two hours to get to know each other here," she said. "There are drinks and snacks over by the back windows. Take this opportunity to make a good impression. Have fun!"

This was one of the things Charlotte had not been looking forward to. She didn't like parties—and the camera crew didn't help.

Dominic came into the room and sat down

in front of the fireplace. Teagan immediately began fluttering her eyelashes at him. "Do you want something to drink?" she asked. Her voice was breathy and Charlotte choked back a laugh.

When Dominic nodded, Teagan went to get him a soda. She swung her hips back and forth, which just made her look ridiculous.

Olivia sat down on the couch next to Dominic. "So why'd you come on the show?" she asked. "I mean, it's pretty obvious what the draw is for us," she giggled, "but since your dad is famous, you could probably date whoever you wanted!"

He looked at her and winked. "What could be better than having the chance to get to know four great girls at once?" he asked.

Seriously, what is with the winking, thought Charlotte. She must have been giving him some sort of look because he met her eyes and said, "What about you, Charlie? Why are you here?"

She managed to smile at him as she said, "I just didn't really have time to date at home.

Besides, a chance to find love and win a scholarship? I'm not gonna pass that up."

Teagan reappeared with a soda for Dominic, dragging Delaney along behind her. "So what kind of things do you have planned for our dates?" asked Teagan. Olivia and Delaney leaned forward a bit, interested. Charlotte played it cool, but she was listening closely, curious to hear what he'd planned.

"You'll see," he said, giving them a sly smile.

I bet he doesn't even know. Catherine probably plans all the dates, thought Charlotte. "Well, I hope you're prepared," she said, raising an eyebrow at him.

"I think you'll find I'm prepared for anything, even you," he replied.

Charlotte hoped this would be over soon. She would have been tense even if this was a private party, but with the camera crews and producers there, she couldn't relax at all. Dominic didn't help matters—she thought he was cute, but the more he talked, the cockier he seemed. He flirted ridiculously with them— even her, a little. It gave her the impression that he thought he was the greatest guy in the world. She couldn't tell if he was really like this or if it was just an act.

She was lost in her own thoughts when she heard Teagan say her name. "Charlie should have washed her face better before she came on TV." Teagan didn't bother to whisper. "She's had her head buried in books for so long, she'll never get the ink off her nose."

Teagan and Dominic both laughed. Charlotte didn't look at them. She could feel herself blushing. *There's nothing wrong with liking books*, she reminded herself, pretending she hadn't heard them. Charlotte turned resolutely to Olivia, determined not to let them get to her. She hoped Dominic only laughed out of politeness, but only time would tell.

Finally after two hours, Catherine called, "Cut!"

Immediately an assistant took Dominic out of the lodge. He gave Charlotte a small smile as he left, and her stomach clenched.

She tried to ignore the tightness in her stomach and wondered if he had a nicer side.

She hoped he did, but he hadn't given her any reason to believe it yet. He hadn't said much to her—Teagan and Olivia hadn't really let the other two girls get a word in. Charlotte was just glad the evening was over. Hopefully things would be different one-on-one.

CHAPTER

5

The next day Olivia woke them all early with a cheerful "Rise and shine!" that made Charlotte want to throw a pillow at her. Grumbling, they slowly made their way out of bed.

Catherine was in the dining hall when the girls arrived for breakfast, but she wasn't eating. Instead she sat at one of the other tables just watching. *She's definitely plotting something,* Charlotte thought.

As soon as they finished eating, Catherine appeared next to their table. "Girls," she said, smiling at them, "no down time today! This afternoon is the first group date. As you know you'll have one every week, and then you'll each have a one-on-one date every week as well."

"What are we going to do?" asked Olivia, clapping her hands with excitement.

"You're going boating on the lake," said Catherine. "Make sure you wear a swimsuit— you'll be water skiing too."

Charlotte perked up a bit at this. She hadn't been looking forward to another group event, but she'd always wanted to try water skiing.

"Will we have to get in the water?" whined Teagan.

"I hate seaweed," added Delaney.

"No one will make you," said Catherine, frowning. "But I strongly encourage you to participate fully in the dates. Dominic chose all these activities, and if you're hoping to make a good impression on him, you should at least try the things he enjoys."

Teagan and Delaney both stared at Catherine with huge eyes. *This will be very interesting*, Charlotte thought, stifling a laugh. "Be ready in an hour," said Catherine. "We'll have sunscreen, food, drinks, all of that. Just bring yourselves!"

As they walked back to their cabin, Teagan said, "I knew I should have gotten a better tan before this!"

"I'm sure it'll be fine," said Delaney.

They changed into their swimsuits right away. Charlotte threw on a T-shirt and shorts over hers, while the other three all wore sundresses. No one said anything about her clothes this time, but she was still self-conscious. It made her angry—at home she never worried about what anyone thought of how she looked, but thinking of the whole country judging her appearance the way Teagan and Delaney had made her anxious.

***

When they arrived at the dock, Dominic was surrounded by members of the crew, who were clearly there to keep them all from interacting before the cameras were ready.

The boat wasn't as big as Charlotte had expected. There was room for only one cameraperson onboard, as well as a driver. A second boat, already loaded with the camera crew, was ready to follow them.

"All right, everyone ready?" asked Catherine. "Let's get started!"

Dominic walked over to the dock, smiling his too-perfect smile. Charlotte still thought it looked fake, but she couldn't help noticing how it lit up his eyes. She hoped she'd see a real smile from him someday. Charlotte followed Teagan, Delaney, and Olivia to him, letting them greet him first.

"You girls ready for some speed?" he asked.

Teagan giggled, though it sounded forced. She hesitated before stepping carefully into the boat. She was pale with fear and her smile looked pained. Delaney nodded, a tentative smile on her face, and Olivia shrieked and jumped up and down. Charlotte just smiled a little and climbed into the boat. "More than ready," she said. Charlotte almost thought she saw an interested gleam in Dominic's eyes, but it was gone in a flash.

They started slowly, cruising around the

edge of the lake, where the cliffs rose high above them. The reds and browns of the rock were beautiful in the sun, and the dark green pine trees at the top of the cliffs looked mysterious and calm.

But the atmosphere in the boat was anything but calm. Teagan seemed to have overcome her anxiety and was back to her outrageous flirting. She removed her sundress almost immediately to reveal a black bikini. Olivia and Delaney followed suit, saying the weather was far too nice to be covered up. Dominic removed his shirt, and as much as Charlotte tried not to look, it was hard to ignore the muscles on display.

"Come on, Charlie, don't you want to join us?" he asked. He winked at her again.

Her stomach flipped at his request—this time his wink seemed charming, and part of her wanted to, but she just shook her head. "I don't want to get a sunburn," she said. "I'll change when we get in the water."

"Then let's get in!" said Dominic excitedly. He got the water skis set up easily. It was clear he'd done it before, and Charlotte admired how confident he was. "Have any of you ever skied?" he asked, looking at each of them. When they all shook their heads, he said, "I'll go first then, and you can all give it a try after you see how it's done!"

He pulled on a life jacket, then strapped on the skis and jumped into the water, whooping at the temperature. He surfaced immediately, shaking water out of his hair.

"Watch how I do this, girls!" he said. The driver passed him the rope and, at Dominic's signal, slowly drove forward until the rope was pulled tight. When Dominic yelled, "Hit it!" the driver accelerated, fast.

Dominic popped up out of the water in a crouch, his arms straight in front of him. The four girls in the boat shrieked at the sudden acceleration and held on. Dominic gave a thumbs-up and the boat sped up even more. Charlotte could see him laughing though she couldn't hear it over the roar of the wind, and she couldn't help but laugh too. Even with the cameras on them, this was fun.

After a few minutes, the driver slowed down and circled back to pick up Dominic. "Who's next?" he asked as he climbed back into the boat.

Charlotte really wanted to go, but Olivia jumped to her feet. "I'll try!" she giggled.

Olivia was terrible. Every time she started to come out of the water, she lost her balance or her feet flew in opposite directions. She tried enthusiastically for ten minutes before signaling that she was done.

"I just can't seem to get the hang of it," she said. She didn't seem upset, though.

"I think it's because you're not bending your knees enough," said Dominic. "You can try again later. Delaney, do you want to go next?"

Delaney agreed, but she clearly wasn't enjoying herself. She seemed scared and tried half-heartedly before quickly giving up.

"Me next," said Charlotte when Delaney had settled back into her seat.

She stood and pulled off her T-shirt and shorts. Her shirt was only halfway off when

Delaney burst out laughing. "I didn't know anyone still bought suits like that!" she said, pointing at Charlotte.

Charlotte was confused. She was just wearing a plain one-piece. She knew it wasn't super fashionable, but she thought it looked nice on her.

"You look like you're on the swim team," said Olivia. She rushed to add, "Not that that's a bad thing!"

Charlotte felt herself blush. It was amazing how bad they could make her feel about things she'd never worried much about. She refused to let it show, though. "I like my swimsuit to stay on when I swim," she said simply. She put on the lifejacket and water skis.

"I don't know why you're worried about that," said Teagan, sneering. "It's not like anyone would want to see what's underneath anyway." Delaney giggled again.

Charlotte dropped into the water. She was angry now, but fighting with Teagan was a bad idea. She already knew that Catherine wanted Teagan to win, and she was sure that when they edited the show they'd make Teagan look good and Charlotte look bad. Six weeks from now she'd never have to see these girls again— she could put up with them until then.

The water was cold, and it cooled off her temper. She grabbed the rope and positioned herself like Dominic had. The tips of the skis rose out of the water in front of her with the rope stretched toward the boat.

"Hit it!" she yelled, and the boat surged forward. The strength of it surprised her, but she kept her arms straight and held on. She felt herself rising out of the water and kept her knees bent. She thought she had it when she suddenly hit a rough patch of water.

Her legs flew apart as she fell, and the rope jerked out of her hands. Bobbing on the water with the life jacket around her chin, she swam awkwardly forward and got ready to try again.

This time, Charlotte was ready. She got her balance right away when the boat pulled her out of the water, and then she was flying. Her legs burned with the effort, but the hours in the gym and at soccer practice paid off.

The boat turned and she zoomed out in a wide arc, bumping over the wake. When she straightened out again, she gave the driver a thumbs-up, asking to go faster. She laughed as they sped up. After a few more minutes, she gave the signal to stop.

When she climbed back into the boat, Dominic was looking at her like he'd never seen her before. "Have you done that before?" he asked. "It took me ages to learn when I was a kid."

"Nope," she said. "I always wanted to, though. Once I got the hang of it, it wasn't so hard." She shrugged and took of the life jacket. "Your turn, Teagan." She passed the wet life jacket over to Teagan, who took it like it was covered in mold.

Teagan complained the whole time she was getting ready. The water was too cold, the rope would hurt her hands, she wasn't strong enough. She only tried because Catherine glared at her from the other boat.

They spent the rest of the afternoon exploring the lake. They ate and drank and skied again several times. By the end of the day, they were all exhausted, but they had managed to get along reasonably well.

Charlotte didn't speak much—she never really knew what to say, and it was even harder with the cameras there. They'd been easy to ignore while she was on the water skis, but on the boat it was impossible. Even though she didn't really talk to him, she saw Dominic looking at her. It made her nervous, even though part of her got a little thrill every time she noticed him looking.

When the sun started going down and the tall cliffs cast long shadows on the lake, the driver docked the boat. Dominic helped each of them out of the boat like a gentleman. "I had a really good time with you all," he said once they stood on the dock. "I can't wait to get to know each of you better during our private dates. Tomorrow I'd like to invite Teagan to come to the beach with me."

Teagan nodded enthusiastically. "I can't wait," she said.

"I'll see you all later," he said. He waved at

them as he walked back toward the trees.

Typical, thought Charlotte. *Of course Teagan gets the first date. It'll be hard for any of the rest of us to make an impression when she's gotten there first.* Even though she wasn't sure how she felt about Dominic, she did want him to like her. If she wanted any chance at the scholarship, he had to.

"Cut!" called Catherine. "Teagan, you'll be picked up at ten tomorrow morning. The rest of the private dates will be Charlie, then Olivia, then Delaney. At the end of the week, you'll film your first confessionals, and then you'll get a day off before the next week of dates begins. When you don't have to film, you're free to explore the area. Just don't get in the way."

A day off, and then a date. I guess it's good I don't have too much time to worry about it, thought Charlotte as she followed the others back to the cabin.

CHAPTER 6

"We had such a strong connection," Teagan gushed. The girls were all lounging in their cabin. Teagan had just returned from her date with Dominic. Apparently it went well. "He even said he'd help me get a record deal!"

"She's an amazing singer," said Delaney.

I guess now we know why she's really here, thought Charlotte.

"And then, when we were lying on the beach, he kissed me," Teagan said. She sighed dramatically and flopped back on her bed. "It was perfect."

"You're telling me he kissed the first girl

on the first date?" said Charlotte. She didn't believe it. She'd watched a lot of seasons of *The One* with Madeline, and there was never any kissing that fast. On second dates sometimes, but never on first dates.

"I told you, we had amazing chemistry. I doubt you'd know anything about that," Teagan shot back.

"I suppose it's possible," said Olivia, though it didn't seem like she believed Teagan either. "Love at first sight is totally a thing."

"Wait, don't you want Dominic to fall for *you*?" asked Delaney, staring at Olivia in confusion.

"Well, yeah, that would be great, if we click and everything," said Olivia. "But only one of us will get that, and I trust the process. Whoever is supposed to end up with him, will." She smiled.

We're in high school, thought Charlotte. *Does anyone actually think Dominic is going to be the love of their life? Or even a long-term boyfriend?* She didn't say any of this aloud, though. It wouldn't change their minds and it would just make them wonder why she was there. If they found out she wasn't sure about being there, Catherine might kick her off the show.

**

The next morning, Charlotte dressed in comfortable clothes. She was told to wear something she could move in that she wouldn't mind getting dirty.

Today she was going on her first date with Dominic. She wouldn't be able to hide behind the others and watch. She hadn't even been this nervous before the state-semifinal soccer game. Her palms wouldn't stop sweating and her hands shook as she put on her mascara. Charlotte hoped she wouldn't make a fool of herself since she'd never been on a date before. Not knowing exactly what Dominic had planned wasn't helping either.

Catherine was all business when Charlotte arrived at the lodge. A car waited off to the side, but there was nothing to give away what she and Dominic might be doing.

"Ready, Charlie?" asked Catherine with a

huge grin that didn't reach her eyes.

She nodded. Catherine gave the signal and the cameras were rolling again. She suddenly felt too aware of her face. Should she smile? Would it be weird to smile at nothing? She didn't want to look angry.

Before she could figure out what to do, Dominic came out of the lodge. He was dressed casually in a jeans and a T-shirt, and his hair was again perfect. Charlotte had to admit he looked good.

"Charlie!" he said, smiling at her. No matter how much people used the nickname, she couldn't get used to it. She was getting better at hiding how much she disliked it, though.

"Hey." She felt ridiculous—she didn't really know what to say to him and the cameras only made it worse. She didn't have much time to think about it, though, because he hugged her. He was taller than she was, and she felt like she was being swallowed by his warmth. It was nice and strange at the same time.

"Let's go," he said, pulling her toward the car.

"Where are we going?"

"You'll see!" he said. "I wanted to surprise you."

Why would you try to surprise someone you don't even know? Charlotte wondered. This could be a disaster.

They drove for ten minutes. Most of the way they didn't talk, which was extra awkward with the cameraperson there. Charlotte pretended to be interested in the scenery outside the window so she wouldn't have to look at either of them.

When she started seeing white fences around pastures, she perked up a bit. "Are we going horseback riding?" she asked, startling Dominic, who had been staring out the other window.

He grinned at her. "Yeah," he said. "I hope that sounds like fun to you." He gave her a shy smile—the most real smile she'd seen from him—and her heart fluttered.

She nodded, smiling back at him.

When they got to the stable, two horses were already waiting for them. Dominic greeted his horse with a gentle pat on the nose. The horse tossed its head excitedly, and Dominic pulled an apple out of his pocket. He offered it to the horse, whispering in its ear. A friendly woman gave them helmets and then adjusted Charlotte's saddle and stirrups before helping her mount. Dominic did all of this himself, looking completely comfortable.

"Have you ridden a lot?" she asked him.

"Yeah, my mom loves horses," he said, patting his horse's neck. "We rode as a family a lot when I was younger."

"I wish I'd been able to do that," she said. "I always wanted to ride horses."

"Well then, I guess it's your lucky day." The cocky smile was back, and he winked at her again. This time she didn't bother to hide the eye roll. He leaned down and whispered to his horse, "I think she might not hate me after all," he said, just loud enough that she could hear. Sitting up again, he teased, "Not that it matters if she hates me . . . I *do* have three other options."

Despite his joking tone, there was enough

truth in his words that they still stung. "Just when I was thinking a guy who likes animals couldn't be all that bad too," she said, refusing to let him see that he'd hurt her.

"What can I say, you bring out the best in me," he teased, chuckling a little.

He nudged his horse and led them onto the riding trail behind the farm. She ignored the camera crew following them on ATVs as best she could and tried to copy the graceful way Dominic sat in the saddle. He moved like the horse was part of him, while she felt like she might fall off at any minute. Still, she was more comfortable than she'd been since the show started. This was even better than learning to water ski.

As they got used to each other, they rode in an easy silence, enjoying the peaceful countryside. Occasionally Dominic stroked his horse's neck absentmindedly. When a butterfly fluttered suddenly out of the bushes at the side of the trail, his horse flinched. "Hey now, you're an awful lot bigger than that little thing," he said calmly to the horse.

"Come on now, don't be scared."

Charlotte smiled to herself.

When they'd been riding for nearly two hours they stopped. They were up at the top of the cliffs that surrounded the lake, and the view was amazing. There were mountains in the distance, still capped with snow even in June. Dominic dismounted and then helped Charlotte off her horse. Her legs nearly collapsed underneath her—she hadn't realized how stiff they'd gotten.

A crew member passed Dominic a basket and a blanket, which he laid out.

"Hungry?" he asked.

"Starving," she admitted.

They began to eat in more silence. Charlotte wished she knew what to say to him, but her mind went blank every time she opened her mouth to speak. She was surprised she didn't feel more awkward, though.

After a few quiet moments, Dominic said, "So what do you want to do after you graduate?"

"I want to be a physical therapist and work

with athletes," she said, relieved that he broke the silence.

"Why not be a doctor, then?" he asked. "You'd make more money."

"And spend more time in school," she said, shaking her head. "I like school, but not that much. Besides, I can't stand blood."

"The daredevil water skier can't stand blood?" he teased. "I never would have guessed that. Guess you had to be a wimp about something."

She shoved him playfully so he nearly fell over. "What about you?" she asked. "Do you want to be an actor like your dad?"

An odd expression of hesitation flashed across his face, but he hid it quickly. The cocky smile was back. "I'd be crazy not to, right?" he said.

She nodded. That wasn't exactly an answer, so she tried a different approach. "What if you couldn't do anything in film or TV? What would you want to do then?"

He looked out over the lake. Charlotte's breath caught as she watched the way the wind ruffled his hair, and she squashed the sudden urge to fix it. "I don't think anyone's ever asked me that," he said, sounding surprised. "I guess I'd have to figure it out."

They finished their meal and continued talking, just trying to get to know each other. After half an hour, Catherine spoke up. "Time to start heading back," she said.

Charlotte had forgotten she was there. She'd never thought it would happen, but she was starting to get used to having an audience.

Dominic quickly wrapped up the picnic supplies and helped her to her feet. He grabbed two leftover carrots and handed one to Charlotte. "Wanna feed them?" He gestured to the horses.

She nodded and followed him over, copying him as he rubbed his horse's nose and offered the carrot on a flat palm. Her horse's lips tickled her hand, and she giggled a little as she looked over at Dominic.

"There you go, beautiful girl," he said softly to his horse. Charlotte smiled, liking this side of him better.

Dominic turned back to her and offered to help her onto her horse. Blushing, she put her hand on his shoulder and stepped into his cupped hands so he could boost her into the saddle. Charlotte settled herself carefully. Her butt was definitely bruised.

"Want to try trotting?" asked Dominic from his own horse. "You can hold on to the saddle."

She nodded nervously.

"Follow me, then. Just nudge your horse a little harder when I start going faster."

Trotting was uncomfortable. Unlike Dominic, who looked totally relaxed, she bounced awkwardly in her saddle. She got used to the strange feeling after a few minutes, and soon she was loving it. The wind and the sun on her face made her feel free. By the time they made it back to the forested part of the trail, she was grinning.

When they dismounted near the barn, she stretched her aching legs as the horses were led back to the stable. "Thank you for today," she said to Dominic, smiling. "It was wonderful.

I'm not going to be able to sit down for a while, but I don't even care!"

He laughed. "If I was allowed to repeat dates, I'd take you again and you'd get used to it."

"You've set the bar pretty high for yourself," Charlotte replied. "I don't know how you'll top this."

"I'll come up with something," he said, his eyes twinkling. "I'll see you at the next group date." He hugged her, lingering a little. Charlotte didn't fight the butterflies this time, enjoying the feeling of his chest under her cheek.

"See you then," she said when she pulled away. She headed back to where two cars were now waiting. They wouldn't ride back together, and she was glad. The Dominic she went riding with was different than the Dominic she first met, and she needed time to think.

CHAPTER
7

Olivia and Delaney also seemed to have fun on their dates, though Delaney didn't really say much. The girls had fallen into a routine in cabin, and while they weren't exactly friends, they could at least talk without arguing. They just tried not to talk about Dominic too much.

Soon the day Charlotte had been dreading finally arrived—confessionals. The girls went up to the lodge after breakfast, where they were taken one at a time to a small sitting room.

Charlotte sat on the couch and looked at the cameras. They were right in her face with this setup, and she'd have to talk straight into them. She'd spent the whole week trying to ignore them, but she wouldn't be able to do that here.

"All right, Charlie, let's get this done," said Catherine briskly. "I'll ask you some questions and you should answer them honestly. We'll edit out the questions later; we just want to get you talking. So, what do you think of Dominic?"

Charlotte figured Catherine wanted her to gush about Dominic, but she wasn't sure how she actually felt about him. Sometimes he was cocky and arrogant, but he was so sweet on their date—she couldn't tell who the real Dominic was. She took a deep breath and played it safe, saying, "He's great. He's so sweet, especially with horses. I can tell he's a caring guy, you know? Plus, he's cute. What's not to like?"

Catherine was looking at her with narrowed eyes. Charlotte could tell she didn't really believe that's what Charlotte thought, but she had no reason to complain about her answer. "So you can see it working out with him?"

"It's still early to tell, but I haven't seen any red flags yet," said Charlotte. She let out a giggle. *Madeline is going to laugh herself silly when she sees this.*

"What about the other girls? How's it going with them?" asked Catherine.

I will not be the girl you turn into the villain, thought Charlotte. *I know what you're up to.* She smiled. "We're doing fine. We're all so different, so it'll be interesting to see who will be the right match for Dominic." *Diplomatic and simple,* she thought. *Hopefully they can't twist that too much.*

"Anything else you want to say? Any problems you see? Anything you didn't like on your date?" Catherine prompted.

"I've had a great time so far!" Charlotte said. "I've always wanted to ride horses, and I loved the water skiing too. I'm just excited to see what else is coming."

"All right," said Catherine curtly. She looked disappointed that Charlotte hadn't said anything juicier. "You're free to go."

CHAPTER

8

They all had a day off at the end of the week.
Only a few unlucky production staff were
left onset to chaperone them. The girls were
bored, and they didn't have their phones to
entertain them.

Charlotte had brought several books to
read, but she was finding it hard to concentrate
in the cabin. Teagan and Delaney were
gossiping on the other side of the room, and
Olivia kept interrupting Charlotte to chat.
She sighed and turned to face the wall. Teagan
stopped talking and looked over at her.

"Why don't you just go somewhere else

to read?" she said. "Or just drop out and go home? Dominic's never gonna pick you. You're too weird."

"Who made you the one who decides who's weird?" snapped Charlotte. "Maybe I think you're weird." *So much for trying to get along*, she thought.

"I heard Catherine say you'll never win," said Teagan. "Delaney was there too. She says you're way too much of a nerd, so she's not going to let Dominic pick you. I, on the other hand, apparently have great potential to make it in the industry."

Delaney nodded in agreement. "Teagan's gonna get a record deal after this, just watch."

"I thought we were all here for a chance to find love," said Olivia, frowning a little.

"I mean, yeah," said Teagan. "But here you also have the chance to break into the entertainment industry. Who doesn't want that?" She laughed, looking at Olivia like she was pathetic.

"But the main point is still to fall in love," insisted Olivia. "There's no way they'll stop him from picking whoever he wants to."

Teagan just rolled her eyes.

Charlotte got up, still holding her book. She'd find somewhere else to read. It was sunny and warm outside, so she'd have lots of options.

She walked along a trail that ran right next to their cabin, admiring the wildflowers that grew near the edges and the tall trees that towered overhead. The trail ran down toward the lake and then followed the shore, giving her little glimpses of the sparkling water through the trees.

She climbed uphill on the rocky path, watching her feet so she wouldn't trip. At the top of the hill was a lookout point with a wooden bench. She wasn't expecting to see someone familiar sitting on it.

Dominic turned to look at her when he heard her footsteps.

"Hey, Charlie," he said, surprised.

"I'm not supposed to see you off camera," she blurted. She didn't like breaking rules. Still, his appearance had her stomach flip-flopping again, and she had to sneakily wipe the sweat off her palms. Charlotte was surprised how pleased she was to see him.

He laughed. "Who's gonna see? There are only a couple people onset today and they gave me a break from filming my confessionals. I don't think any of them are going to come up here."

"Still, I should probably go," she said, turning to walk back the way she'd come.

"Please don't," he said quietly. It was a different tone than she'd heard him use before, and she stopped. He sounded shy—more like the guy who whispered to his horse than the cocky player she'd seen around the others.

"Will you sit with me?" he asked.

She hesitated for just a moment before joining him. She could feel him looking at her, but she didn't meet his eyes. They sat in silence for a few minutes, listening to the birds.

"I'm sorry I've been a jerk," said Dominic suddenly.

She looked at him in surprise. "What?"

"I didn't want to do the show," he confessed, looking at his hands. "My dad thinks college is a waste of time. That I should just go into the entertainment business like him and my mom. We've obviously got connections. He won't pay for college, and I can't get financial aid because my family is . . . well-off. This was the compromise."

"I didn't know you got a scholarship too," Charlotte said before she could stop herself.

"If the producer's are pleased with our performance, we do," Dominic explained.

"So by coming on the show, you get a scholarship and you get your name out in the industry," Charlotte said, nodding. "Why does that mean you have to act like a jerk, though?"

"Catherine told me I had to make sure the ratings were good and suggested that the audience likes a bad boy. I don't want to screw up my shot for college, so I figured I'd try it."

"Well, if you're just pretending, maybe your dad is right and you should become an actor. You do jerk really well." She felt a little sorry for him, but she wasn't going to let him completely off the hook. When he looked ashamed, though, she felt a tiny bit guilty.

"I know I shouldn't do it. I'm kind of stuck now, though. At least it's only five more weeks."

"And you get to do all sorts of cool things," Charlotte said. She nudged his elbow with her own. "Though I guess they probably aren't as exciting for you as they are for me. You've probably tried most of them before. We'd have to do something crazy like skydiving to find something you haven't gotten to try." She laughed awkwardly.

He shuddered. "No way. No heights. I do not need the whole country to see my knees shaking."

"Really? You're scared of heights?" she said, standing up. "So if I go stand over here . . ." She walked to edge of the cliff, grinning at him.

"Don't do that!" he hissed. His voice sounded higher than usual. "Please, Charlie, just . . . get away from the edge."

She backed up and glanced at him. He definitely looked scared. "I won't do it again as long as you don't call me Charlie off camera anymore," she said.

"What do you mean? That's your name."
He looked confused, and Charlotte thought
the wrinkle in his forehead was adorable.

"It's a nickname—one that I hate.
Catherine insists I use it because it's more
relatable or something." She rolled her eyes.
"It's stupid. I've always gone by Charlotte."

"Charlotte," he said, testing it out.
"That fits you better." Then he grinned
mischievously. "You better hope I don't screw it
up on camera now."

She laughed. "I'm sure you can remember.
Charlie and Dominic-the-jerk can go on
their dates, and Charlotte and Dominic can
have actual conversations offset. In secret,
obviously." She blushed when she realized she
had basically just asked him to sneak around
to see her. She hadn't meant to do it, but this
version of Dominic seemed so much more real
than the guy on the group dates.

Dominic didn't say anything for a second.
Charlotte thought she could see a slight flush
on his cheeks and he gave her a shy smile that
made her heart skip. She was confused. Could

Dominic really be this different off-screen? How was she supposed to know which one was the real him?

"Are you serious?" he asked, fidgeting nervously. "Maybe we could meet on our next day off? It's nice to talk to someone without everyone watching. You can see Catherine plotting all the time."

Charlotte wrinkled her nose at the mention of Catherine. "Tell me about it. But if we get caught, I'm blaming you," she said, teasing. "We have to be careful, though. I don't want to get sent home—you might be the grand prize, but you're not the only prize. I could use that scholarship too."

"Now I know your real motive," he laughed. "It's okay, I get it. I hope you're not pretending to be into me just to try and get the money, though." He laughed again, but this time it sounded strained. He was clearly worried that someone might actually do that to him.

Charlotte reached out to squeeze his hand, surprising both of them. "I'm not that good an actress. But if it turns out you're not into any of us and you wanted to pick me just so I could get the money, I'd keep your secret." It was her turn to wink obnoxiously at him.

His laugh was relaxed again. "Let's just see how things go," he said. "We can come back to that later if we have to."

She realized they were still holding hands at the same time he did. They both looked at their clasped hands and froze. She tried to pull away, but he tightened his grip just slightly. Charlotte was flustered. She could feel him looking at her, but she didn't meet his eyes until he gently tilted her chin up with his free hand. Her heart raced and she could feel her cheeks burning.

"I'll let you know where to meet before our next day off," he said.

She wanted to ask how he'd manage that, but she couldn't seem to speak. Instead she just nodded.

"I've got to get back. Dominic-the-jerk will see you tomorrow for the group date," he said, chuckling.

She smiled at him. "See you tomorrow."

Charlotte watched his broad shoulders disappear around the bend in the trail and then sat back down on the bench, finally pulling out her book. Even after the hints of a different Dominic on their first date, this was not how she'd expected things to go.

CHAPTER
9

The next two weeks passed quickly. The group dates were more fun as they all got to know one another, even though they couldn't forget that they were competing. Dominic continued his cocky persona during filming, and sometimes he was so convincing that Charlotte thought she'd imagined their accidental meeting.

He had managed to slip her a note during their second private date—a hike—and they'd met up again on their day off. Since Catherine was around that day and quick to notice if he disappeared for too long, it had been a short meeting. Still, it had been nice to talk in private, and Charlotte wanted to get to know that version of Dominic better. *Her* version, she kept catching herself thinking.

Their on-screen interactions hadn't changed much on the outside, but they felt different to Charlotte. They felt a lot more like flirting. She also found herself fighting feelings of jealousy when she watched the other girls with Dominic. She kept reminding herself that he couldn't just ignore them. He had to follow the rules as much as she did. But she couldn't help worrying that he might like the other girls too. Charlotte's feelings confused her, but she was starting to think she might actually like him—a lot.

This week—their third on set—he asked her to meet him at the overlook after dinner the night of their confessionals. He hoped they'd have a little more time since they would be done filming by then. If they were careful, they would have several hours together.

Charlotte was nervous. She hadn't spent this long with Dominic anywhere except on set, where they were both playing roles. She wouldn't have that to hide behind now and hopefully he wouldn't be hiding either. She was always a little worried that the nice version of Dominic was as much of an act as the guy he played on-screen.

The girls walked back to the cabin after dinner. Teagan had been glaring at Charlotte all through the meal, and she had no idea why. While they didn't like each other, they hadn't fought lately.

"Is there a problem, Teagan?" Charlotte finally asked.

"Why are you even here?" Teagan snapped, like she'd been waiting to say this for ages. "You don't seem into the show, and you don't even seem to like Dominic. If you don't want to be here, why are you staying?"

"Just because I don't act like you doesn't mean I don't like him," said Charlotte. "Not everyone has to be so obvious about everything."

"I think you're only here for the money," said Teagan. Olivia was looking back and forth between them, clearly uncomfortable.

Charlotte managed to keep her expression blank. Even if her main motivation for coming on the show had been the scholarship, she wasn't opposed to finding love. And the side of Dominic she was seeing when they were alone was making that option look better and better. Besides, it wasn't any of their business why she was here.

"I think you should quit," said Delaney, chiming in. "The rest of us are here to find love, and so is Dominic. It's not fair to him or us for you to stay when that isn't what you want."

That's what you think, thought Charlotte. But she was too angry to be smug about knowing the real reason Dominic had agreed to be on the show—or about her own budding relationship with him. "How would either of you even know what I want?" she asked. "It's not like you tried to get to know me. From the beginning, you decided I was weird because I'm not like you and that was it."

"Come on, let's just calm down," said Olivia. "I'm sure Charlie is hoping Dominic is the one for her as much as the rest of us, so—"

"Just shut up, Olivia," said Teagan. "No one wants your sunshine and rainbows right now."

"I'm not staying to listen to this," said Charlotte, and she walked out of the cabin. Her cheeks were hot with anger, and she could feel her hands trembling. Hopefully everyone—including her—would calm down before she got back. She was supposed to meet Dominic anyway, and this was as good an excuse to leave as any.

The shadows were starting to lengthen as she walked up the trail to the lookout. It was a calm evening, and the forest was peaceful. She felt herself relaxing as she let the sounds of nature wash over her.

Dominic was already at the overlook when she arrived. The evening sun was golden, and it shined on his dark, wavy hair. She stopped and just looked at him for a moment. After a moment, Dominic turned to look at her. The genuine smile on his face drove away the last of her anxiety. "Hey."

"Hey," she replied, walking over to sit down next to him on the bench. She sat closer than necessary, but he didn't seem to mind. She felt like her blood was fizzing—the aftereffects of her anger combined with the fresh air and the feel of Dominic's body heat beside her.

"Did something happen?" he asked. "You look sort of intense."

"It's just stupid drama," she muttered. "You don't want to hear about it."

"Let me guess—Teagan," he said, smiling a little.

She looked at him sharply.

"Oh, come on, I'm not blind," he laughed. "She loves drama. And she clearly doesn't like you."

Charlotte laughed too, relaxing. "Yeah, well, all of us living together isn't ideal."

"What'd she say?"

She shrugged. "The usual—that I'm too weird for you to like me. They accused me of only being here for the scholarship. Well, excuse me for not being rich enough to be able to ignore fifty thousand dollars." Her stomach tightened when she remembered how nasty they'd been.

"That's stupid," he said. "I'm rich, and I think it's a lot of money." He cocked his head curiously. "And what do you mean, the usual?"

"They all think like that. Except maybe Olivia. I'm not into fashion like they are and I like school and stuff, so obviously there's no way a guy like you would want me. Even Catherine has said it. You've seen the girls do it during dates."

He looked upset at that. Charlotte smiled. "It's fine. I can take it. You've got to play your character and I have to play mine." *I just hope we can remember which parts are real.*

"I don't think you're weird," he said, nudging her leg with his. She felt the touch like an electric shock, and his kind words sent a rush of warmth through her.

"Just don't go saying anything to anyone. You'll blow our cover," warned Charlotte.

"I know," he said. "I can't wait 'til this is over."

"It'll be strange to go back to normal life," said Charlotte. "I hope people aren't too weird about it after the show airs." She shuddered at the thought of everyone at school staring at her.

"They'll definitely be weird," he said. "Once you're even a little bit famous, they forget you're a person. Just look at how Teagan acts around me."

"Ugh. You better pick me, then. I'll need that scholarship to make this worth it." Her laughter was dancing in her eyes, and she could tell he wasn't offended.

He reached out and caught her hand in his, entwining their fingers. Her breath caught in her chest. "I don't think you really need to worry about that," he said.

Suddenly she couldn't control the butterflies in her stomach, and she couldn't meet his eyes. The sun was setting over the lake now, and they watched it together, holding hands and enjoying the silence.

When the sun disappeared below the horizon and the red sky melted into blues and purples, Charlotte tried to stand up. "They'll notice if I'm not back soon," she said. But Dominic wouldn't let go of her hand.

"Stay a little longer," he said quietly. "The stars are coming out."

The look in his eyes made her pause. "Just a little while," she said finally, smiling and sitting back down. She hadn't really wanted to leave, anyway.

They talked late into the night, and Charlotte loved how easy it was. The sky was black and sparkling with stars when they landed on the subject of music. "You like *country*?" asked Charlotte, shocked.

"Classic stuff, like Johnny Cash," he said quickly. "Not most of the new stuff. And it's not the only thing I like. Though I don't know why I feel like I have to justify my music taste," he laughed. "There's nothing wrong with it."

"I guess the old stuff is a little better," she said, shrugging. "It's just not my thing."

"You're one to talk. You still listen to nineties boybands," he teased.

"I like the harmonies," she said, blushing a little. Dominic chuckled.

After a few quiet moments, he said, "Come down here." He slid onto the grass and laid back. "It's really clear tonight. You can't see this many stars in the city. It was always my favorite thing about camping."

She lay down on her back next to him, gazing up at the sky. He was right. The sky looked like black velvet. More stars than she'd ever seen in her life winked at them.

"It's beautiful," she said. "But it makes me feel small."

"That's what I like about it," he said. "When my dad's around, everyone always acts like we're the most important people in the world. But we're not. He's just a guy who's good at playing pretend for other people to watch. This kind of thing," he gestured up at the sky, "reminds me that I'm just as insignificant as everyone else."

"I don't think you're insignificant," Charlotte said softly.

He turned his head to look at her. "You're not insignificant either."

When she turned to face him, she realized their faces were only inches apart. She was glad it was too dark for him to see her blush. She felt trapped by his eyes. Slowly, unconsciously, they closed the distance. It was a gentle kiss, just a soft press of lips, but Charlotte felt it to the tips of her toes.

She looked at him for a second, speechless. "I've never done that before," she said, blushing even harder.

Dominic gave her a shy smile, and she could tell part of him was pleased to hear this. "Then I'm even happier I didn't do it in front of the whole country," he said quietly. "We shouldn't have to share it."

Charlotte suddenly felt flustered. She didn't think their kiss would have felt like that if he was acting, but now things seemed like they were moving too fast. This was new territory for her. She didn't know how to respond to him when he talked like that. "I should go," she whispered.

He smiled and stood up with her. "I'll see you tomorrow," he said.

Charlotte glanced back at him as she walked toward the cabins. She could tell he was still watching her, his eyes hidden by the shadows.

***

It got even harder to go back to their fake on-screen personalities after the kiss. Charlotte could only hope she didn't blush every time he looked at her, and she did her best to behave the way she had in the beginning. Sometimes she felt his eyes on her, though, and she caught herself watching him too.

They managed to sneak away several times over the fourth and fifth weeks of filming, sometimes on their day off and sometimes after filming had ended for the day, but Olivia was getting suspicious. She'd started asking Charlotte where she was going every time she left the cabin, and Charlotte wasn't sure how many more walks Olivia would believe she was taking.

Later in the fifth week, they were the only two in the cabin. Delaney and Teagan were still at dinner.

"You're up to something," Olivia said, out of nowhere.

"What?" asked Charlotte. Her stomach clenched, but she tried to act like she had no idea what Olivia was talking about.

"Where do you go all the time on those walks?" she demanded.

"Nowhere," Charlotte insisted, though she couldn't help feeling a bit bad for lying. "Really. I just wander around—there's no other way to get away from everyone else."

Olivia narrowed her eyes. "Well you always come back from your walks looking awfully happy for someone just wandering around alone."

"Just because you love talking all the time doesn't mean we all do," Charlotte snapped. "Liking walks and being alone isn't against the rules." She turned away. Olivia was annoyingly observant sometimes, but Charlotte felt a bit sorry for her. After all, Olivia was the only one who was nice to her—and she seemed to be the only one genuinely interested in finding love on the show.

Olivia dropped it, but she watched Charlotte closely over the next few days. On their next confessional day, Charlotte saw Olivia talking to Catherine. Charlotte was too far away to hear anything, but both of them looked at her as she walked toward the lodge for her turn. *It's probably nothing*, she thought. *Olivia can't prove anything.*

CHAPTER
10

Charlotte and Dominic had been sneaking away more and more often. The more they got away with it, the less careful they were. Even with Olivia watching them, Charlotte hadn't been able to stay away. The thrill of Dominic's company was intoxicating, and she craved the way she felt both safe and a little out of control around him.

They had just finished filming their week five confessionals, and she'd walked down to the dock behind the lodge. She sat on the dock with her feet dangling in the water. Dominic sat next to her, pulling her close to his side.

"Everyone should be busy with the other confessionals for a while longer," he said.

She turned to look at him. His eyes were dancing in the sunlight. He leaned down to kiss her, and she put her arms around his neck.

"Oh, by all means, don't mind me," said a sharp voice from behind them.

They sprang apart and turned around, looking up at the cold expression on Catherine's face.

"You signed a contract. You know you're not allowed to see him off camera," she said to Charlotte. "The only reason you are not packing your bags right now is because I don't want to deal with recasting your role." Charlotte stared at her feet, embarrassed that they'd been caught and angry with herself for being so careless.

The producer turned her attention to Dominic. "And you. No one wants to see you end up with someone like her. Teagan is the perfect girl-next-door. The viewers will love her. So get your act together and do your job."

Dominic stared back at her in disgust. "I

agreed to come on the show. I did not agree to pick someone I don't like just because you think the viewers will like it better. Teagan is mean, and we have nothing in common. I don't want anything to do with her." He turned to Charlotte. "Go on, Charlotte. You should head back to the cabin. You don't need to hear this."

Charlotte gave him a look of silent thanks and hurried off. Instead of going back to her cabin, though, she hid behind the trees just out of their view. She wanted to hear what else Catherine had to say.

"You will pick who I say you'll pick," she said when she thought Charlotte had gone. "Plus, you know the rules. If I don't like your performance, you can bet you won't get that scholarship."

Charlotte thought she could see his body tense up, but Dominic kept his voice even. "What does everything have to be about money? Sometimes it seems that's all my dad cares about too." He crossed his arms over his chest. "Why can't this show actually be about finding love?"

Catherine laughed nastily. "That's just the way the world works, so get used to it. But since you mentioned your dad . . ." She paused for a long moment. "If you don't pick Teagan, I can make sure he never gets another role. I have a lot of power in this industry, you know."

There's no way she has that much power, Charlotte thought. But the sudden fear on Dominic's face made her nervous.

"Wait, hold on," Dominic choked out. "This scholarship is really important to me, and you can't punish my dad for my actions."

Catherine took a step closer to him. "You have no idea what I can do. So I guess you have to decide what is more important to you—your future and your family, or Charlotte."

Dominic nervously raked his hands through his hair and stared at his feet. Charlotte's heart dropped into her stomach.

I can't listen to any more of this, Charlotte panicked. She took one more look at Dominic, wishing she could reach out and comfort him.

Instead she snuck quietly back to the cabin, her heart breaking with every step. Charlotte didn't know what Dominic would do. She didn't want him to lose his scholarship or hurt his dad's career just for her, but a bigger part of her prayed he'd choose her anyway.

CHAPTER

11

Two days later, everyone gathered for the final group date, which was bowling. The lodge had two lanes in the basement, and Dominic told the girls he wanted to have a more casual date. Though this bowling alley was a lot fancier than Charlotte was used to, it still reminded her more of a real life date than most of the dates they'd gone on for the show.

The five of them shared one lane. There had been a short but intense argument about whether to put the bumpers up—Charlotte thought it was cheating, while Teagan insisted she'd never manage to roll anything other than a gutter ball without them. Teagan won.

Charlotte really didn't care that much, but she'd been in a bad mood since Catherine had caught her with Dominic. Her mood didn't improve when Dominic refused to meet her eyes when the girls arrived for the date. He greeted them all as a group, but he didn't look at her once. Even Dominic-the-jerk didn't ignore her. He teased her and tried to flirt with her in the most obnoxious way possible, but he'd never pretended she wasn't there.

She tried not to think about Catherine's threats, but the way Dominic was treating her made her nervous that he'd made his choice— and that it wasn't in her favor.

Charlotte smiled at him, trying to catch his eye, but he just kept talking to Delaney, bending his head toward her as if he was completely fascinated. The smile slipped off Charlotte's face, and she sat alone on one of the small couches.

She took the third turn at bowling. The walk to the lane felt much longer than it was, and Charlotte could feel eyes on her back. She could hear whispering, but she couldn't make out what was said. She picked up her ball, trying to ignore them.

Suddenly she heard an explosion of giggles and then, "It was her first kiss?" Teagan's screech rang out above the sound of the music playing.

Charlotte froze. She couldn't believe it. He'd told them about their kiss? Her embarrassment rose hot through her body. She couldn't turn around to face them. She was afraid she might cry if she looked at Dominic. Instead she took deep breath and bowled.

She barely saw the pins fall. She could still hear the laughter echoing in her ears, but she willed herself to face them and finish the date, imagining that her spine was ice. *He isn't worth it*, Charlotte told herself. *I should have known better than to trust the kind of selfish jerk who goes on a dating show so he can date four girls at once.*

The rest of the date passed in a blur. She let her eyes skate over Dominic like he didn't exist. Two could play that game. Catherine frowned at her from behind the cameras, silently urging her to participate more, but Charlotte refused to act like everything was okay.

Afterward, she followed the other three back to their cabin, but she didn't go in. Instead she sat on the ground behind it, leaning against the rough logs. *After the way he acted tonight, there's no way he's going to pick me*, she thought miserably. Charlotte knew he was trying to protect his family and his future, but it still hurt. Tears blurred her vision, turning the stars into streaks across the night sky.

"Charlie?" said a quiet voice.

Charlotte didn't look at Delaney. "My name's Charlotte," she snapped.

"Sorry, I didn't realize you hated it that much," said Delaney. Charlotte was surprised that she actually sounded sorry.

"What do you want?" she asked. "Are you here to laugh at nerdy, inexperienced Charlotte some more?" She tried to sound angry, but her voice broke and it just came out sounding pathetic.

"No, I swear. Look, Charlotte, I'm really sorry. I know I've been mean, and I wish I could take it all back." Delaney sat down next to her.

Charlotte was stunned—Delaney had played a very convincing mean girl. "Then why'd you do it?" she asked. "I never did anything to you."

"I don't know." Her voice was small. "If anyone knew it was wrong, it was me. People are always mean to me at school because I'm so shy," she said. "I guess I thought if I stuck close to Teagan, she wouldn't pick on me."

Charlotte finally looked at her. "I thought you were so strong," continued Delaney. "I figured you could take it because you always stood up to us and never let it get to you."

"Well, it did get to me," said Charlotte.

"I know. I'm sorry. I never meant to make you feel like this. It was awful of me," Delaney said quietly. "Will you forgive me?"

There was a long silence. Charlotte wasn't sure if Delaney really meant it, but she figured it didn't matter anyway. Slowly, Charlotte nodded. "Okay." She was silent for a few more moments before blurting out, "I've been

sneaking around with Dominic off camera."
She couldn't keep it in any longer—not after
the emotional day she'd had.

"Wow," said Delaney. "I didn't even think
you guys liked each other as friends."

The whole story spilled out of Charlotte,
from the first accidental meeting to their first
kiss to Catherine catching them.

"Honestly, I'm impressed," Delaney said
when Charlotte had finished. "It was gutsy to
go behind Catherine's back."

Charlotte snorted. "Or stupid."

"Probably both," said Delaney, laughing
a little. "For what it's worth, I don't think
Dominic was lying to you. On my one-on-ones
with him, he never seemed interested at all.
Like, he wasn't mean to me or anything, but
there just wasn't anything there. He's never
kissed me."

"You aren't the only other person he's
seeing, though," said Charlotte.

"Yeah, well, I know Teagan talks like she's
got him wrapped around her finger, but she's
faking it. He hasn't kissed her either. I think

Olivia would have told us all immediately if anything was really clicking with her and Dominic, so there's probably nothing going on with them either."

"You don't seem very upset about him not being into you. Don't you want to win?" Charlotte asked curiously.

"Nah," said Delaney matter-of-factly. "I'm here because my mom made me apply. She always wanted to do something like this."

Charlotte winced. "I'm sorry."

"You don't seem like the type to be on a show like this either."

"My best friend sent in my application as a joke," said Charlotte, rolling her eyes. "I only agreed to come because I could really use the scholarship. And I thought it might be an interesting experience." She paused. "Plus, there was a little part of me that hoped maybe Dominic and I would fall for each other."

"Well, I guess you sort of got two of the three. It has definitely been interesting, and it seems like you fell for him. Or at least with the Dominic who acted so differently away from the cameras," said Delaney. "It's too bad you can't be sure how he's feeling."

"I mean, I know Dominic says he's different, but I'm not sure I can trust that. How do I know Catherine wasn't actually in on it all? Maybe they were just making more drama." Charlotte laughed bitterly.

"Don't write him off just yet," said Delaney. "You don't know what else Catherine said to him. Anyway, even if he turns out to be awful, you only have to get through one more week and you can talk to me whenever. I can't stand Teagan any longer."

Delaney got up and headed back into the cabin. Charlotte sat for a little while longer, enjoying the fresh air and trying to decide if Delaney really meant it. She wanted to believe her, but she'd already been hurt once by someone she thought she could trust. *Only one more week.*

CHAPTER 12

Dominic gave Charlotte a stiff hug when he arrived at the dock for their last one-on-one date. The final one-on-one dates were different—this time the girls got to pick what they wanted to do. And Charlotte had taken full advantage of that.

"I cannot believe you picked this," he whispered low enough that the cameras wouldn't pick it up. She just smiled at him. Charlotte thought parasailing sounded awesome.

"Aren't you excited? This is going to be so fun!" she said, climbing into the boat. His eyes flashed before he hid the expression behind a bland smile.

The boat sped out into the middle of the lake. The driver stopped and strapped them into life jackets and the harness. When they were all set up on the back of the boat, he released the parasail to catch the wind. The driver made sure they were ready and then sped up.

They rose steadily into the air, the water getting farther away as the wind whipped their faces. Charlotte whooped and laughed. She'd never done anything so exhilarating before. Beside her Dominic was tense, his hands clenched so hard the knuckles were white. His attempt at a smile looked more like a grimace.

Serves you right, thought Charlotte, ignoring his fear.

She'd picked parasailing for three reasons. The main one was that she'd wanted to try it, and she didn't think she'd get another chance anytime soon. The fact that it scared Dominic was the second. And the last reason was that they didn't have to talk—the wind was too loud in their ears for them to hear anything, so she let herself relax and enjoy the ride.

When they finished and were back in the boat, she asked, "Wasn't that great?"

"It was a rush," he said, clearly unsure about the experience.

"An amazing one!" It was obvious that Dominic didn't want to talk about his fear of heights on camera. "You seemed kind of tense, though."

"Well, I wasn't," he growled. "I was just cold. It was windy." A dark blush was rising in his cheeks, and she grinned innocently at him.

They sat in silence for the rest of the ride back to shore, despite the producers' best attempts to get them talking. Charlotte didn't know what to say to him now, and Dominic didn't seem interested in talking either. The longer the silence went on the larger the seed of guilt in her gut grew.

Catherine frowned at them both when they got off the boat but just said, "Go get changed and come back to the lodge for confessionals.

We want to get your reactions to these final private dates while everything is fresh."

***

Charlotte still hated filming confessionals. She had to do them every week, but they didn't get easier. All those people watching her and asking her personal questions—it was her worst nightmare.

"All right, let's get going," said Catherine as Charlotte settled on the couch. "Charlie, how do you think that final date went?"

"Well, *I* had fun," she said. "You'll have to ask Dominic what he thought; he didn't say anything to me."

"You sound mad at him," said Catherine. There was a glint of excitement in her eyes.

Screw it, Charlotte thought. "He's been a bit of jerk during this whole show, honestly. I don't know what I expected from a guy who comes on a dating show—I guess you could say the same thing about the girls, but at least we're all only dating one guy at a time." Charlotte huffed. "Anyway, he's so arrogant.

He loves himself too much to ever let anyone else in. Every time I've thought I might be getting closer, he's done something to make me question it."

Catherine had to know Charlotte wasn't talking about their on-screen dates anymore, but she didn't stop her. "And then he goes and makes fun of me to the other girls." She felt the anger leave her, only to be replaced by the hurt she still felt. She glanced down at her folded hands. "That was kind of the ultimate betrayal. I always tried not to bring up the other contestants to him—that's going too far. All I could do was build our relationship and hope it was enough, and clearly it wasn't."

Looks like Catherine gets what she wants, thought Charlotte as she walked back to the cabin after her confessional. She couldn't believe she'd let herself think, even for a moment, that she might be able to have a real relationship with Dominic.

CHAPTER

13

The final episode was filmed in the great
room of the lodge where they'd first met
Dominic. Even Charlotte had dressed up,
wearing the only nice dress Madeline had been
able to talk her into bringing. It was simple
and fitted, but the deep purple complemented
her eyes.

When they were all settled in the great
room, Dominic arrived. He wore a suit that
fit him perfectly and looked like he'd stepped
off the red carpet. Charlotte stamped on the
butterflies in her stomach at the sight of him.
She was furious with herself for still reacting to

him that way, and she couldn't wait until this was all over.

"Tonight is the night," he said. "I don't want to wait any longer. I know who the one for me is, and I hope she feels the same way." Charlotte noticed Teagan beaming at that. She tried not to roll her eyes.

Dominic continued. "I met someone here who made me feel like a normal guy for the first time in my life. She didn't even seem to like me much at first."

Wait, what? Charlotte thought. Her eyes snapped over to Dominic in surprise, but he just kept talking.

"But I made a mistake—I listened to the producers here. I let them tell me who was right for me, even though I knew they were wrong. I hurt the girl I care about because I didn't stand up for myself—or for her. The producers wanted me to pick Teagan, but she's not the one for me. Charlotte is."

"Charlie?" cried Teagan, outraged.

"Charlotte," said Dominic firmly. "Her name is Charlotte. And she was my first kiss too, so you can all stop laughing at her for having her first kiss with me."

Charlotte froze at those words. *Did he really just admit that on national TV for me?* She looked up shyly, finally believing that maybe he really meant what he was saying.

His eyes were flashing as he looked at Charlotte. She had forgotten how to speak and was just staring at him. Before she could figure out what to say, Catherine spoke. The producer's face was pale with suppressed rage.

"Dominic, we talked about this," she said with fake sweetness in her voice as she stepped onto the set. She smiled widely at the camera, as if trying to remind him they were there. "Charlie is not the right choice. Teagan is perfect for you!"

"No," insisted Dominic. "I want Charlotte."

"Are you sure you know what you're doing?" she hissed, clearly trying to regain control of the situation while the cameras were still rolling.

"I'm not gonna let you blackmail me," Dominic said. "You can't force me to choose your pick just because it will give the show better ratings."

The other girls gasped, and Catherine looked horrified. She glanced anxiously at the cameras. "I—I don't—"

"You're going to air the finale as filmed, or I quit," Dominic said over her. "You won't get your perfect ending with Teagan. In fact, you wouldn't get any ending at all. I'm sure the network will love that."

"You're trying to force him to pick someone he doesn't want?" said Olivia, frowning. "This is supposed to be a chance at love. He's found it and you're trying to take it away."

"Oh grow up, you stupid girl," said Catherine. "This was never about love. It was about good TV."

"I think this is great," said Delaney, smiling at Charlotte. "They make a great couple."

"You traitor," spat Teagan, glaring her. "I can't believe you're doing this to me!" She burst into tears and stormed off the set.

Catherine finally seemed to notice the cameras were still rolling and threw down her clipboard. "Oh, for crying out loud," she grumbled to herself, clomping off in her tall heels.

Charlotte smiled at Delaney. "Thanks," she whispered.

Delaney just grinned and pushed her gently toward Dominic. The camera crew kept filming them, but as Charlotte looked over at Dominic, she felt everything else in the room disappear.

He walked over to her and pulled her into a tight hug. She pressed her face against his chest, trying to prove to herself that this was real. "You're . . . you're really picking me?" she asked. "Even after everything Catherine said to you about your dad?"

Dominic frowned. "I didn't know you'd heard that. I didn't know what to do at first, but I realized I didn't want to hurt you. I'm sorry that the others found out about the kiss. I didn't mean to tell them—they just figured it out and everything got carried away before I could stop it."

She nodded. "I'm sorry too."

"After seeing how upset you were on our last date, I knew I couldn't go through with what Catherine wanted. I'll be fine, my dad will be fine. None of the other stuff matters."

Charlotte laughed. "Well, she still technically got her ending."

He nudged her chin up and kissed her once, then smiled at her. "Guess we're both going to college," he said. "And . . ." he pulled away to dig out something from his pocket.

Charlotte gasped as he held out a ring with a tiny jewel in the center. The promise ring. "There's this, if you want it," he said.

She closed her hand around it but didn't put it on. Instead, she leaned up onto her toes to kiss him again. "I've already got the scholarship," she said. "And you. I've already won the grand prize."

ABOUT THE AUTHOR

When she isn't traveling, Claire Ainslie lives
in Wisconsin with her two cats, Bonnie
and Eejit, where she spends too much time
planning interesting futures for herself. She
enjoys baking (because she enjoys eating),
Irish dancing, soccer, and fresh air. If you
can't find her, it's because she's lost in a book.

Escape!
The Island
The One
The Right Note
Treasure Hunt
Warrior Zone

MASON FALLS MYSTERIES

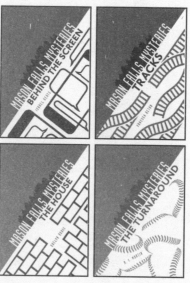

EVEN AN ORDINARY TOWN HAS ITS SECRETS.

Becoming Prince Charming

Family Business

Next in Line

A Noble Cause

Royal Pain

Royal Treatment

**THE VALMONTS ARE NOT YOUR
TYPICAL ROYAL FAMILY.**

HAVING A SUPERPOWER IS NOT AS EASY
AS THE COMIC BOOKS MAKE IT SEEM.

CHECK OUT ALL OF THE TITLES IN
THE

SUPER HUMAN

SERIES

THE DO-OVER

THE ACCIDENT
THE CHEAT
THE DATE
THE GAME
THE LIE
THE PRANK